KRANG'S
SPACE RAID

Written by Stella Paskins
Illustrated by Rod Vass
assisted by Maria Keane

Carnival

An Imprint of HarperCollins*Publishers*
77-85 Fulham Palace Road,
Hammersmith, London W6 8JB

Published by Carnival 1991

Teenage Mutant Hero Turtles™
© 1991 Mirage Studios
Licensed by Copyright Promotions Ltd
text © 1991 HarperCollinsPublishers

ISBN 0 00 192563 6

All rights reserved

Printed in Great Britain by
BPCC Hazell Books, Paulton and Aylesbury

"Wowee! Cowabunga!" yelled the Teenage Mutant Hero Turtles as they set off on holiday. Since Donatello had finished his improvements to the Blimp Airship they couldn't wait to try it out on a really long journey. Now they were going to visit their friends, the Punk Frogs, who lived in the Okeefenokee Swamp, several hundred miles south of New York.

"This thing really moves since you souped up the engine," shouted Leonardo over the wind that whistled about them.

"This is nothing," Donatello yelled back. "We could even go to the moon if I really opened up the throttle."

"Florida will do nicely for now," commented Raphael, clutching at his bandana for fear it would fly off.

"Yeah," agreed Michaelangelo. "Like - I've never fancied the moon. No atmosphere!"

After a while, Donatello began looking around. "Can anybody see the swamp yet?" he called. "We should be pretty near by now."

"I can see something brown and patchy, with a couple of green blobs," remarked Michaelangelo.

"Huh?" Sure enough, instead of floating over the marshy paradise that the Turtles had been dreaming of, all they could see was a vast patch of baked mud, cracking in the heat.

"Maybe we took a wrong turn," said Raphael. "There's no water near here."

"Impossible!" replied Donatello. "According to my calculations we should be right above the swamp, *now*."

"Let's go down for a closer look," suggested Leonardo.

The Blimp Airship dropped and the Turtles swept their eyes around the barren landscape. Suddenly Michaelangelo started. "Whoa! Y'know those green blobs I saw? Well - they're the Frogs!"

Sure enough, there were Atilla, Ghengis, Napoleon Bonafrog and Rasputin the Mad Frog, once victims of the same mutagen that had transformed the Turtles, and now their firm friends.

The Turtles wasted no time in swinging down from the Blimp as soon as it was low enough. The Frogs were lying on the ground, gasping and almost unconscious. Ghengis managed to open one eye as Leonardo leaned over him. "Hey, pal, what's happened?"

Ghengis licked a dry tongue round cracked lips, then spoke in a hoarse whisper. "Our swamp - it's dried up. We haven't had any water for days now."

Raphael and Donatello had been checking the other Frogs while he spoke. "These guys are almost totally dehydrated," said Raphael.

"There's only one thing for it," decided Leonardo. "We must take them back to our sewer and hope that Master Splinter will be able to help."

If the journey to Florida had seemed fast, Donatello made sure that the return was even speedier. The Blimp wasn't really built for so many passengers, but somehow they managed and before long they were back in New York.

Splinter was waiting for them at the entrance of their secret hide-out. "I sensed that you might not be away long, my students," he said, as the Turtles helped their sick companions into the room. "There have been bad reports on the television."

While their teacher examined the Frogs, the Turtles tuned in to Channel 6 for the latest news. It wasn't long before their close friend, ace reporter April O'Neil, appeared on the screen.

"Meteorologists are still baffled by the disappearance of large areas of water all over the United States. All the major reservoirs are empty and now whole lakes, swamps and rivers appear to be drying up. The government has asked that everyone ration their use of water while the problem is being investigated."

Donatello switched off the TV. "This is serious."

In a hidden cavern, just under the outskirts of the city, the noise of pumps only barely masked the sound of dripping. Two sinister figures overlooked a huge vat which was steadily filling with water.

The masked figure turned to his companion. "Well, Krang, I hardly expected this pea-brained scheme of yours to work. It seems I was wrong for once."

The wrinkled brain creature from Dimension X, Krang, glared out of the belly of his robot exoskeleton. "The trouble with you, Shredder, is that you don't think BIG. Soon my Hydro-extractor will have removed the last trace of water from the country and I'll have it here, concentrated, to do with as I wish."

Bebop and Rocksteady, Shredder's personal henchmutants, overheard the alien's boasting. "You wanna be careful," announced Bebop. "There's a water shortage. I heard it on the news."

Shredder swiped an armoured gauntlet at the semi-warthog, which Bebop hastily ducked. "You fool - we're *causing* the water shortage." He turned back to Krang. "I sometimes think those two have water on the brain."

April also had water on her mind. After leaving Channel 6, she had decided to head for the local water reservoir to carry out some background research.

Soon she was outside the gates and was reading the sign hung there. "Reservoir. Closed until further notice." She got out of her van. "Oh well, I can still do a little fact-finding. Who knows - I might even come across something that the experts missed."

Clutching her portable recorder, April opened the gates and started to look around the area. While she was staring at the vast, empty reservoir that had once held the city's water supply, she became aware of a strange hum beneath her feet.

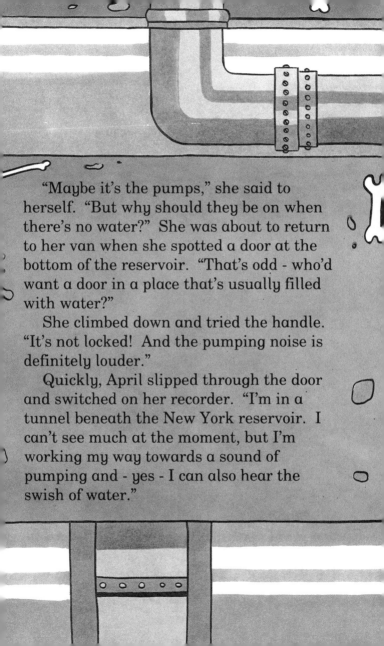

"Maybe it's the pumps," she said to herself. "But why should they be on when there's no water?" She was about to return to her van when she spotted a door at the bottom of the reservoir. "That's odd - who'd want a door in a place that's usually filled with water?"

She climbed down and tried the handle. "It's not locked! And the pumping noise is definitely louder."

Quickly, April slipped through the door and switched on her recorder. "I'm in a tunnel beneath the New York reservoir. I can't see much at the moment, but I'm working my way towards a sound of pumping and - yes - I can also hear the swish of water."

April kept up a running commentary
into her recorder. Eventually the tunnel
widened into a cavern - the same cavern
where Shredder and Krang were collecting
the stolen water.

April's eyes widened at the sight before
her - Foot Soldiers were swarming all over
the underground hollow and the roof
flickered eerily, reflecting the ripples from
the liquid below. On a dais above the main
water vat she could see Shredder and Krang
operating a control panel. "Oops - I think
I'd better call for some back up," gasped

April, fumbling for her Turtle Com and reversing up the passage.

She had hardly time to press the bleep on the device when it was knocked from her hands and smashed into smithereens against the wall of the tunnel. At the same time her portable recorder was snatched from her shoulder and it fell to the ground.

April spun round to see the leering faces of Rocksteady and Bebop grinning at her. "Nice of you to drop by," said Rocksteady. "Krang says he hasn't got any tea, but would you like a glass of water?"

13

Back at the Turtle lair, Donatello was looking puzzled. "That bleep *must* have been April trying to call us. But she's not on any of the frequencies."

"It must have been an accident," said Raphael.

"Maybe," replied Donatello, " but she's not answering my calls either."

"Don't sweat it, Donatello," said Michaelangelo. "Come and have some celebration pizza." He was sitting among a pile of pizzas trying to tempt Napoleon to take a bite.

"It's no good," Napoleon was saying, "we still don't like pizza."

The Frogs were now fully recovered thanks to Splinter, a bath and several large glasses of precious water. Donatello joined the group. "I'm sorry, but I can't help worrying about April."

Splinter rested his bony paw on his pupil's shell. "Enjoy yourselves while you can, my students. Our water supply has just dried up and I fear we are now all in great danger."

Raphael threw down the pizza slice he was eating, making Michaelangelo wince. "I *can't* just sit here, waiting to dry up!"

Atilla and the other Frogs nodded in agreement. "At least we should try and do something."

"You're right," said Leonardo. "And I think I know where to start - the reservoir!"

"But surely that's empty," objected Raphael.

"Does anyone have a better idea?" sighed Leonardo.

In no time, Michaelangelo was at the wheel of the Turtle Van. The Frogs and the rest of the Turtles all piled in the back.

As they neared their destination, Donatello pointed. "Look, there's April's van. She must have had the same idea as us."

"I can't see anyone about," remarked Rasputin. "Perhaps you were right about your pal being in trouble."

Leonardo nodded. "We'd better be real careful."

The eight friends clambered out of the van. "Let's split up," said Ghengis. "We'll cover more ground."

So, each Turtle paired up with a Frog and began to explore. Barely ten minutes later, six of them had regrouped with nothing to report.

"Has anyone seen Donatello and Atilla?" asked Leonardo.

Just then they heard a low whistle from the bottom of the empty reservoir. They looked down to see Donatello and Atilla standing by the secret door. In Donatello's hands were April's portable recorder and the smashed Turtle Com.

Krang's prisoner had no idea that the Turtles were so near and she was quite frightened, although she refused to show it.

Krang and Shredder couldn't resist showing off. "I expect you're wondering what I'm going to do with all of this water," gurgled Krang.

"How about a brainwash?" retorted April.

"Very funny," hissed the alien, "but you'll laugh on the other side of your face when you see *this!*" Krang pressed a couple of buttons and his monitor lit up. On the screen there was a strange dome-shaped interior unlike any April had seen before. It contained Foot Soldiers working on large vats, similar to those in the cavern.

"Where on earth is that?" she asked.

"Nowhere on *Earth*," chortled Krang.

"It's on the moon!" He and Shredder laughed at the look on April's face. "You will soon be experiencing the lunar delights of Moonbase Krang for yourself, but there is something more important to do first!"

Krang nodded at Shredder, who deftly flicked some switches on the console. The roof of the cavern slid back, revealing the darkening New York sky. Right overhead April could see the pale disc of the full moon. "Now!" shouted Krang.

Shredder once more turned to the console. At the press of a button, the water in the largest vat shot skywards in a long, endless stream. "What are you doing?" shrieked April.

"Look at the monitor," instructed Krang. Water was swirling into the vats in Moonbase Krang. "Soon all the water I have acquired will be safely collected on the moon. Eventually I shall have control of all the water in the world - then I shall be ruler of Earth indeed!"

"Not if we have anything to do with it!" April gasped as the Turtles and Frogs leapt into the cavern, knocking stray Foot Soldiers flying. A fierce fight broke out, but the eight brave challengers had no trouble overpowering every encounter.

Krang's menacing tones broke through the noise. "Stop your battling, you buffoons. The Hydro-extractor is a delicately balanced piece of equipment. If you upset it, your planet's puny inhabitants can say goodbye to their water for ever!"

"And don't forget we have your precious April O'Neil as hostage," added Shredder.

"You won't have her for long!" snarled Raphael, catapulting towards the dais. While he was still in mid-air the flash of a dimension portal stopped everyone in their tracks. When Raphael landed on the platform it was empty.

"Huh - where are they?"

Krang's voice oozed from the monitor. "As you can see, we have now transported safely to the moon and the portal has closed behind us. Soon April will make the broadcast of her life - informing everyone that the water supply is now under *my* control."

Shredder's masked visage pushed its way into vision. "So Turtles, finally you're all washed up!" he gloated, and the screen went dark.

Donatello turned from his investigation of the Hydro-extractor.

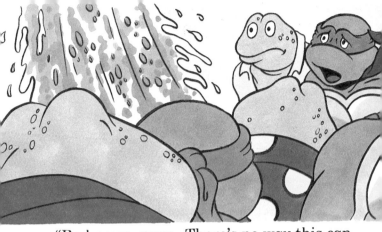

"Bad news, guys. There's no way this can be dismantled safely. The control must be in Moonbase Krang." Dismally the Turtles and Frogs surveyed the river of water, still spiralling moonwards and seeming to take the very essence of life with it.

"If only we could somehow get to the moon," said Rasputin. "We'd soon sort out that pink pumpkin and his cronies."

Donatello slapped his brow. "But we *can!* In the Blimp!"

Suddenly things didn't seem so bleak. "You mean, what you said about the Blimp being fast enough to go to the moon was for real?" said Michaelangelo.

"Well, I'd have to adjust the gas pressure and reinforce the skin," pondered Donatello, "but, sure, speed is no problem."

"What're we waiting for!" whooped

Napoleon. "Let's go go GO!"

"Wait a minute," said Donatello. "I'll
have to go alone. The Blimp must carry as
little weight as possible, and I'm the only
one who's got the remotest chance of
dismantling that Hydro-extractor."

"But someone's got to watch your back,"
remarked Ghengis. "I think one of us
should go with you." Eventually Donatello
agreed and, as everybody volunteered to go,
they drew lots to decide.

"Far out!" cheered Raphael, winning the
draw. "Shall I bring back some green
cheese for your pizza, Mikey boy?"

"C'mon - back to the sewer," ordered
Donatello, heading for the surface and the
Turtle Van. "You'll have to sort out some
pressure suits, while I finish modifying the
Blimp."

23

While Donatello and Raphael were gone, time hung heavily with those left behind. In the hours that followed, they cleared the area of all stray Foot Soldiers, checked that the reservoir was fully secure from the outside and listened to updates from Splinter on the Turtle Com.

After a while Donatello appeared on the small screen. "We're off now. Wish us luck - the Turtle Com will be out of range up there." It was frustrating for the others not to be able to watch the Blimp take off for the moon, but Splinter assured them that all had gone well and they were safely on their way.

The water flowed, on and on. Tired of the constant pumping swish and the ache of waiting, Michaelangelo idly rested his head on his arm and played with the buttons on Krang's deserted monitor.

Quite by chance, he was surprised by a hum that swiftly crackled into a fuzzy image. "Whoa - satellite TV!" he exclaimed.

Pleased for a diversion, the others all gathered round. "Better than that," breathed Leonardo. "You've picked up the direct line to Moonbase Krang."

"Look," shouted Ghengis. "There's Don and Raph! They did it!" But the cheers of joy were short lived.

"Those Foot Soldiers are sneaking up on them," cried Atilla, "and they have no idea." Half a dozen green fingers grappled on the console, trying to find some way of communicating a warning to the innocent Turtles on the moon, but it was no use.

Too frustrated to watch the picture any more, Leonardo turned his eyes to the column of water. "Maybe we *can* help," he proclaimed.

His friends looked at him expectantly. "We're good swimmers, aren't we? And where is that vertical river going?"

"Straight to the moon!" smiled Napoleon. "We just have to jump on board and hitch a ride!"

"Not you guys," ordered Leonardo. "This could be a one way trip. Michaelangelo and I'll deal with this." And with cries of "Turtle Power" the Turtles plunged into the flow and were whisked upwards.

Ghengis looked at the other Frogs. "Not us, eh? What is it those Turtles say?" And with a cry of "Cowabunga" the Frogs followed their friends into the water chute.

The attempt to sabotage Krang's moonbase was not going to plan. Donatello and Raphael were outnumbered by several Foot Soldiers, not to mention Bebop and Rocksteady. April could only watch helplessly as her friends were rounded up.

Just as everything seemed lost, Leonardo and Michaelangelo burst out of the incoming water, like jets from a water pistol. In the next instant, the four Frogs shot out behind them. "All *right*," shouted Michaelangelo. "Time to boogaloo!"

"What?" roared Krang at the surprise intrusion. April instantly kicked Krang's robot feet from under him, and he fell forward on to Shredder. The low gravity slowed down the fall and April laughed as Krang, followed by Shredder, then Bebop and Rocksteady, all toppled like dominos in syrup.

The Turtles and Frogs enjoyed the feel of the low gravity, which made the fight look like an underwater ballet. The Foot Soldiers didn't stand a chance.

Suddenly there was a joyful shout from Donatello. "I've found the reversal controls!"

Leonardo spun to face Krang. "OK you bag of brains. Give yourself up."

"Never!" Once more there was the flash of a dimension portal - and the villains were gone.

The Turtles and the Frogs cheered Donatello until April's voice broke through the uproar. "I hate to break up the party, guys, but how are we gonna get home?"

The green team looked at each other, then turned to Donatello. "Hey - have I ever let you down?" he laughed.

Their mechanical genius explained that when the Hydro-extractor was reversed, the moon river would remain for a while, but in reverse - gushing towards the Earth. "April, you'll have to have Raphael's pressure suit and come back with me on the Blimp," he continued. "There's no way you could stand the pressure otherwise."

He turned to the Hydro-extractor again. "OK you guys - GO - before the water chute disappears." His companions didn't need telling twice.

April must have passed out on the return journey, for when she opened her eyes she found her feet firmly on solid ground. It was pouring with rain, and everyone was drenched but smiling.

Splinter was looking after her while the Turtles and Frogs appeared to be loading up the Blimp with luggage.

"What are you doing, guys?" she asked.

"Going on holiday - like we planned in the first place," replied Leonardo.

"What? In this rain?" April just had to laugh along with the Frogs and Turtles when she realised what she'd said.